Tall Tales

Story by Chris Bell
Illustrations by Mini Goss

PM Chapter Books
part of the Rigby PM Collection

U.S. edition © 2001 Rigby
a division of Reed Elsevier Inc.
1000 Hart Road
Barrington, IL 60010-2627
www.rigby.com

Text © Chris Bell 2000
Illustrations © Nelson Thomson Learning 2000
Originally published in Australia by Nelson Thomson Learning

06 05 04 03 02 01
10 9 8 7 6 5 4 3 2

Tall Tales
ISBN 0 7635 7446 5

Printed in China by Midas Printing (Asia) Ltd.

Contents

Chapter 1

Pen Pals

Martin's Bay School

Martin's Bay, MI 48356

Dear Anna,

Today our teacher, Mrs. Tam, told us we had to have pen pals. She made us pick names out of a hat. Guess what? I got you. My name is Philip and I'm nine years old.

From, Philip

Philip sat looking at what he had written. Why did I have to get a girl for a pen pal? he thought. What will I write about to a girl? Girls don't like soccer or anything that boys like.

Philip hoped they would only have to write once. But Mrs. Tam wouldn't let them get out of it that easily.

Mrs. Tam waited for all the children to hand in their letters. "I'll mail these to your pen pals' school. Next time you can write to your pen pals' home addresses," she told the class.

"This is a great way to make new friends," said Mrs. Tam. "And it will be good exercise for your brains."

I've got plenty of friends. And I get enough exercise playing soccer, thought Philip.

Chapter 2

Anna

Redwood School
Redwood, MI 48032

Dear Philip,

I'm nine years old, too. Our teacher, Mr. Alonzo, says we have to write every week for the whole semester. So I'll try and tell you some things about me.

We live in a big house with eight bedrooms. I have a pet chimpanzee. She has a bedroom of her own. Do you have any pets?

From, Anna

19 Seaview Road
Martin's Bay, MI 48362

Dear Anna,

We have a dog named Jex. He lives in a doghouse in our backyard.

I have a little sister who's a pain. Her name is Laura.

I can't think of anything else to write.

From, Philip

P.S. Do you walk to school?

54 Forest Hill Street
Redwood, MI 48039

Dear Philip,

My dad works for a big company. He goes away a lot on business. When he is home he takes me to school in his helicopter.

Where are you going for vacation? We're going to our vacation home in Hawaii.

From, Anna

Chapter 3

Philip Uses His Imagination

The next week in writing class, Philip sat staring at the blank paper in front of him.

"Philip," said Mrs. Tam, looking over his shoulder, "Why haven't you written anything? Tell your pen pal something interesting."

Philip mumbled, "I don't have any interesting things to write."

"Well, use your imagination," said Mrs. Tam.

19 Seaview Road
Martin's Bay, MI 48362

Dear Anna,

I forgot to tell you something in my last letter. My dad is a famous race car driver. We go all around the country to watch his big races. He has a whole room full of trophies and prizes.

From, Philip

"Let me read your letter, Philip," said Mrs. Tam at the end of writing class.

"Uhh ... it's not finished," said Philip.

It was no use arguing. As Mrs. Tam read the letter, her mouth grew into a tight line. "I think you should start again, Philip. And this time, use a little less imagination. You can rewrite it for homework."

On his way home, Philip passed a mailbox. He thought about the letter in his pocket. He thought about the new letter he was supposed to write for homework.

It didn't really matter. Mrs. Tam had said to use his imagination. He could just mail this letter now. No one would ever know.

Philip looked around and pushed the envelope into the mailbox.

Let's see what you think of that, Miss Rich and Famous!

Chapter 4

Weekend News

54 Forest Hill Street
Redwood, MI 48039

Dear Philip,

　We've been very busy. On the weekend, we went sailing in our yacht. The captain caught fish for dinner, and we dined at the captain's table.

　What did you do on the weekend?

From, Anna

19 Seaview Road
Martin's Bay, MI 48362

Dear Anna,

It was hot here on the weekend. We went swimming in our pool. After the chef served us lunch, we rode our motorbikes.

Dad was not racing this weekend.

From, Philip

P.S. What is your chimp's name?

54 Forest Hill Street
Redwood, MI 48039

Dear Philip,

My chimp's name is Jancy. We got her when we owned a circus. That was great fun. We used to have all sorts of animals and special acts.

I really liked flying on the trapeze. It was scary with no net.

From, Anna

19 Seaview Road
Martin's Bay, MI 48362

Dear Anna,

It sounds really cool at your place. I'd love to come and meet your chimpanzee. How about I come over one weekend?

Can your dad take me for a ride in his helicopter?

I'd invite you here, except we're having some building work done.

From, Philip

Chapter 5

A Few Changes

The next day at school, Mrs. Tam announced, "Since it is nearly the end of semester, I have a surprise for you all. Mr. Alonzo, from Redwood School, and I have arranged a picnic day. He will bring his class here. We will have a soccer match and other games. And you will all get to meet your pen pals."

All the children looked excited. All except Philip, whose face turned bright red.

Oh no, he thought, I can't meet Miss Rich and Famous here. She might ask all sorts of awkward questions.

Philip was worried. But then he had a sudden thought: Maybe I'll get lucky and be sick on picnic day! If not, what am I going to do?

54 Forest Hill Street
Redwood, MI 48039

Dear Philip,

My dad has sold his helicopter so I won't be able to take you for a ride now.

We're also moving to a smaller house. But you can still write to me at the same address. I'll get the letter.

Maybe I could come to your house instead?

From, Anna

19 Seaview Road
Martin's Bay, MI 48362

Dear Anna,

We've had a few changes, too. My dad has given up car racing. Mom said it was too dangerous at his age.

By the way, I might not get to see you on picnic day. I'm going to be pretty busy playing soccer and things.

Don't worry about asking for me. I'll come looking for you.

From, Philip

Chapter 6

Picnic Day

The day of the picnic arrived.

When the children put on their name tags, Philip wadded his up and put it in his pocket.

While the children ate lunch, Philip picked up litter, and while they played games, Philip helped in the school kitchen.

Then it was time for the soccer match. And Philip still hadn't seen Anna anywhere.

Now all he had to do was get out to the soccer field without being seen.

Phew! He'd made it. So far, so good. While he was playing soccer, he would be safe. And after the game, maybe he could help Mrs. Tam, or pick up litter again.

Anything to stay out of the way.

As the game started, Philip was so lost in thought he nearly didn't see the ball heading straight for him. Just as he took the pass, someone else moved in and took the ball from him. Philip fell and slid along the ground.

"Wow," gasped Philip. "What a great tackle," he yelled to the other player.

"Thanks. It was good, wasn't it?" asked the … girl.

A girl?

"What's your name?" asked Philip, as he stood up.

"Anna," replied the girl. "What's yours?"

"I'm Philip," he said grinning. "Hey, I didn't know you played soccer."